Author: Casey W. Christofferson
Project Manager: Zach Glazar
Editor: Jeff Harkness
Swords & Wizardry Conversion: Jeff Harkness
Art Direction: Casey Christofferson
Layout and Graphic Design: Charles A. Wright
Cover Design: Charles A. Wright
Cover Art: Adrian Landeros
Interior Art: Adrian Landeros
Cartography: Robert Altbauer
Fantasy Grounds Conversion: Michael G. Potter

FROG GOD GAMES
ISBN: 978-1-62283-869-1

FROG GOD GAMES IS:

Bill Webb, Matthew J. Finch, Zach Glazar, Charles A. Wright, Edwin Nagy, Mike Badolato, John Barnhouse

TABLE OF CONTENTS

The Tower of Jhedophar

Introduction

The Tower of Jhedophar is a ***Swords & Wizardry*** adventure designed for four to six characters of 8th to 10th level, although it is easily scaled for higher or lower levels with slight modifications. For suggestions on how to scale the adventure, see the **Scaling the Adventure** sidebar. The adventure has several difficult traps that only a skilled thief may bypass or remove. It is therefore suggested that at least one character be a thief, and that the party also include one cleric, and one magic-user. The remainder of the party should consist of frontline fighters.

Background

The Tower of Jhedophar was once a great school of magic where the arch-mage Jhedophar trained many of the age's greatest magic-users in the arcane arts. Times changed — as did Jhedophar — and as the half-elf finally felt the weariness of age creep into his bones, he began frantically to strive as many wizards do for means to unnaturally lengthen his life. Such is the fate of wizards to possess the power to bind planes and the mysteries of existence with words, alchemy and the secret numbers that are the root of the universe. Vexing it must be to have so many wonders to discover yet only a limited lifespan with which to uncover even greater knowledge.

Jhedophar was once a great hero who with the aid of Lord Tork and other great heroes wrested the *mandrake staff* from the witches of Stench-Hollow Downs. Many adventures did he have, the strange *mandrake staff* figuring greatly in the building of his legend, and some say that the fame of his exploits indeed contributed to the success of his school of magic. At some point, however, something changed in Jhedophar, turning his heart to evil. Some say it was the power of the *mandrake staff*, while others claim it was contact with a dark force he discovered while walking the planes of creation.

For whatever reason, 800 years ago, or so the legend says, Jhedophar wrought a great ritual within the summoning chamber of his tower and made contact with a being of pure evil whose will and mind were greater than his own. There, Jhedophar was granted immortality in un-death by the might of this unspeakable power. Jhedophar signed and sealed the pact with the blood of his very own apprentices.

Always fearful of thieves, Jhedophar constructed a great covered labyrinth around the base of his tower, girding it from outside intrusions. This labyrinth that guards the entrance to the tower is nearly as legendry as the tower itself, having been the bane of many a treasure seeker or would-be plunderer of the secrets that Jhedophar hath wrought within his eldritch fortress.

Beyond the construction of the labyrinth and the sealing of the great portal, little is known of what goes on within the gleaming tower. It is believed that Jhedophar is a great traveler of the planes and a frequent visitor to the City of Brass. Speculation being what it is, one fact remains: Jhedophar was the bearer of the *mandrake staff*, a unique staff said to possess unlimited power in the hands of its wielder.

Synopsis

Having heard of the great wonders hidden within the Tower of Jhedophar, the characters seek out the structure to plunder its vast resources of magical knowledge and to destroy the powerful evil which the very existence of Jhedophar represents. The characters travel a great distance through tangled wilderness or over rough and stormy seas (at the discretion of the Referee) to finally reach the fabled Tower

of Jhedophar. Once there, they enter the Labyrinth of Jhedophar that girds the tower's exterior. The characters face down new adversaries and traps before they enter the tower's forbidden portals and peruse its secrets.

After encountering undead creatures known as **spellgorged zombies**, the characters finally face Jhedophar, where the lich attempts to dissuade them from destroying him by asking the characters to rid him of a red dragon that has taken up residence in his labyrinth. The characters may have already made the same deal with the dragon, who is attempting to gain the fabled *mandrake staff* for himself!

Upon completing the adventure, the characters gain a new powerful magic item and knowledge of new magical spells. It is possible the characters may gain the sword known as *Karelis*, a weapon that may be used by the Referee as a seed for further adventure.

Adventure Hooks

The characters may find their way to the Tower of Jhedophar by various routes. Since it has no set location, you may insert the Tower of Jhedophar into your campaign wherever you desire. It could be located in an evil city, in a ruin, on an island, in a lost jungle, or high up on a mountaintop. Any wilderness adventures of appropriate difficulty to lead the characters to the tower are the domain of the Referee. Listed below are adventure hooks designed to get the characters immediately involved in the adventure.

- While traveling from one place to another, the characters discover they are passing close to the Tower of Jhedophar.
- Villagers beseech the characters to go forth and destroy a dragon that is laired within the cursed Tower of Jhedophar. They tell of a band of heroes who went forth over a month ago to slay the dragon but never returned.
- A treasure map describes a fabulous magical item called the *mandrake staff* and its supposed location in a place called the Tower of Jhedophar.

• A cleric is sent by his religious order to bring back the *mandrake staff* from the clutches of Jhedophar so that its power may be investigated. This plot device works equally well for magic-users, who are sent instead by their guild. Alternatively, a magic-user's guild could send the characters to seek revenge on Jhedophar for murdering his apprentices.

• A paladin's order or ranger's troupe sends the characters out in search of the lost sword *Karelis* that is said to have belonged to the famed knight known as Lord Tork. The sword is destined to help thwart a great evil soon coming to the world.

THE LABYRINTH OF JHEDOPHAR

The labyrinth of Jhedophar was constructed to keep would-be thieves from bothering his delicate arcane studies. It serves as the lair to his undead minions and protectors such as Nazoj the demiurge and E'elaim the crypt thing. The mature adult red dragon Exeterus also makes his home here but is actually an uninvited squatter that has taken up residence in the western side of the labyrinth. The characters must navigate this dangerous labyrinth to find the actual entrance to the Tower of Jhedophar, possibly enlisting the aid of the spirits and monsters within the labyrinth to accomplish their goal. Of course, we all know that's not going to happen, and the characters will instead crawl from this adventure covered in blood and gore.

A broad disk-shaped structure girds the base of the Tower of Jhedophar. A solitary pair of solid bronze double doors 20ft wide in the southern face of the tower appears to be the only entrance. Like the tower itself, the sides of the disk are as smooth as glass, affording no handholds. The entire surface of the central tower and the disk around its base give off a strange luminescence that seems to change with the play of light from the sun and moon.

THE LABYRINTH OF JHEDOPHAR

Entrances and Exits: Area L-1 in the south of the tower complex; roof opening in **Area L-11.**

Wandering Monsters: The animated remains of many unlucky adventurers scour much of the labyrinth in search of food. Roll 1d12 once every 30 minutes the characters spend within the labyrinth.

1d12	Encounter
1	1d4 wraiths
2	1d4+1 bloody bones
3	1d2 spectres
4	1d2 ghouls
5	2d4 four-armed gargoyles
6	1d4 barrow wights
7–12	No encounter

Barrow Wights (1d4): HD 6; AC 3[16]; **Atk** slam (1d4 + energy drain); **Move** 12; **Save** 10 (+1 save in labyrinth); AL C; CL/XP 10/1400; **Special:** insanity gaze (30ft range, save or affected by *symbol of insanity* as spell), level drain (1 level with hit, slain creatures rise as barrow wights in 1d4 rounds). (*The Tome of Horrors Complete* 595)

Bloody Bones (1d4+1): HD 5; AC 3[16]; **Atk** 4 tendrils (save or held), 2 claws (1d6); **Move** 12; **Save** 11 (+1 save in labyrinth); AL C; CL/XP 7/600; **Special:** resistance to fire (50%), slippery, tendrils (10hp, AC 3[16], save or held). (*The Tome of Horrors Complete* 63)

Four-Armed Gargoyles (2d4): HD 4+1; AC 3[16]; **Atk** 4 claws (1d4), bite (1d6), gore (1d6); **Move** 15 (fly 24); **Save** 13; AL C; CL/XP 6/400; **Special:** +1 or better magic weapons to hit, freeze (hard to spot). (*The Tome of Horrors Complete* 263)

Ghouls (1d2): HD 2; AC 6[13]; **Atk** 2 claws (1d3), bite (1d4); **Move** 9; **Save** 15 (+1 save in labyrinth); AL C; CL/XP 3/60; **Special:** immune to charm and sleep, paralyzing touch (3d6 turns, save avoids). (*Monstrosities* 191)

Wraiths (1d4): HD 4; AC 3[16]; **Atk** touch (1d6 + level drain); **Move** 9 (fly 24); **Save** 12 (+1 save in labyrinth); AL C; CL/XP 8/800; **Special:** +1 or better magic or silver weapons to hit, level drain (1 level with hit). (*Monstrosities* 518)

Spectres (1d2): HD 6; HP 42; AC 2[17]; **Atk** spectral touch (1d8 + level drain); **Move** 15 (fly 30); **Save** 10 (+1 save in labyrinth); AL C; CL/XP 9/1100; **Special:** +1 or better magic weapons to hit, level drain (2 levels with hit). (*Monstrosities* 445)

Shielding: The labyrinth is shielded from teleportation and dimensional travel "into" it. However, it is not shielded from teleportation "*out*" of the labyrinth. Jhedophar may enter and exit the labyrinth as he pleases, which is to say, he does not, traveling directly to his chambers in his tower and avoiding the goings on within the labyrinth altogether.

Continuous Effects: The entire labyrinth is affected by Jhedophar's evil and receive +1 bonus to all saves. Any creature slain within the labyrinth rises as a bloody bones in 1d6 rounds unless spawned by an undead creature. Creatures *raised* or *resurrected* before the 1d6 rounds pass do not transform into undead.

Standard Features: Unless otherwise noted, all doors within the labyrinth of Jhedophar are locked and made of bronze. Nazoj the demiurge (**Area L-10**) and E'elaim the crypt thing (**Area L-17**) hold *wardstones of Jhedophar* that open all the doors inside the labyrinth and the tower.

The tower obviously cannot be climbed without magical means. Characters choosing to climb using *frozen concoction* or who *levitate* or *fly* to the top of the disk note that the roof is broken along the southwestern edge of the disk. The disk is 270ft in diameter and 20ft tall, with the tower rising from the center of the disk itself.

The entry portals are solid bonze and locked with a *wizard lock* spell and a mechanical lock.

L-1. Entrance Chamber

The entrance chamber is barren except for glowing words inlaid with silver upon the back wall of the chamber. Exits are to the east and west.

When read, the writing on the wall instantly transforms into a tongue the reader easily comprehends.

It says: "Be gone fools who tread within the labyrinth of Jhedophar, from here my tower door is too far. Sad it was the day you chose to invade my home and thus here forever will reside thy bones."

As soon as the characters enter the labyrinth, Jhedophar casts *wall of iron* over the doorway to block their escape. He has been scrying their progress with his *crystal ball*.

L-2. Bloody Bones

Sitting on the floor throwing dice and gambling over a pile of gold coins are 5 bloody bones. They attack when the characters enter the chamber.

Bloody Bones (5): HD 5; **HP** 37, 35, 34x2, 31; **AC** 3[16]; **Atk** 4 tendrils (save or held), 2 claws (1d6); **Move** 12; **Save** 11 (+1 save in labyrinth); **AL** C; **CL/XP** 7/600; **Special:** resistance to fire (50%), slippery, tendrils (10hp, AC 3[16], save or held). (*The Tome of Horrors Complete* 63)

Treasure: The bloody bones have 300gp that they have been passing back and forth to one another as they mindlessly gambled away the ages.

L-3. Spiked Pit Trap

Stepping on a floor plate in this corner triggers a **spiked pit trap**. Characters must roll below their dexterity on 4d6 to avoid falling into the 20ft-deep pit. Anyone who falls in takes 2d6 points of damage from the fall and lands on 1d4 spikes that do 1d4 points of damage each.

L-4. Trapper

A large, ornately carved chest sitting in the center of this broad, irregularly shaped room is a trapper.

The creature waits until the majority of the party crosses into the center of the room to open the chest.

Trapper: HD 12; **HP** 87; **AC** 0[19]; **Atk** buffet (1d8+1); **Move** 6; **Save** 3; **AL** N; **CL/XP** 14/2600; **Special:** resistances (cold, edged or piercing weapons, fire) (50%), smother (to-hit roll, wrap around creature, automatic buffet damage, suffocate and die after 2 x constitution rounds), surprise (1–3 on 1d6). (*The Tome of Horrors Complete* 564)

L-5. Ten Pin Alley

A trapped floor plate triggers a magical trap Jhedophar set long ago while he was in one of his crueler moods. The plate triggers a hold person spell trap that affects every creature within a 10ft radius. Within seconds, a giant stone ball hidden behind an illusory wall to the north rolls down the hallway, crushing all within its path. Creatures who fail the save vs. hold person are stuck in place and automatically take 10d6 points of damage (no save) from the rolling ball. Characters who resist the charm must still roll below their dexterity on 4d6 to jump out of the ball's path or take 10d6 damage (although they can make a saving throw for half damage).

L-6. Crypt of Lord Tork

Rotting tapestries depicting the great deeds of a long-dead warrior hang in this chamber. A large stone sepulcher carved in the likeness of the warrior buried within dominates the room. A glint of shining metal can be spied upon the ground next to the sepulcher, hidden among the remains of a broken armor rack set up to hang the tack and harness of a mighty warhorse.

One round after characters enter the chamber, the sepulcher's lid slides free and the bones of Lord Tork rise from his tomb. In life, Lord Tork was a great hero, a cavalier without measure among the horsemen of his age. He was also Jhedophar's ally and swore to protect the wizard for all the days of his life. He even granted Jhedophar the land upon which the tower is built. However, Lord Tork never expected the depths to which the wizard's greed and lust for knowledge would take him. When word came that Jhedophar sealed the school and slew his apprentices, Lord Tork rode forth upon his valiant steed Jasper to challenge the wizard. The vigilant Jhedophar was prepared for the aging hero, however, and slew Lord Tork, binding his soul to a circlet of gold. Jhedophar now controls the poor hero's bones from his scrying chamber, forcing the long-ago hero to serve as a guardian to the wizard's lair.

Lord Tork, Skeleton Warrior: HD 12; **HP** 92; **AC** –1[20]; **Atk** *+3 bastard sword* [*Karelis*] (1d8+9); **Move** 12 (30ft leap); **Save** 2 (+1 save in labyrinth); **AL** C; **CL/XP** 12/2000; **Special:** +1 or better magic weapon to hit, fear aura, find target, immune to turning, magic resistance (60%). (*The Tome of Horrors Complete* 495)
Equipment: *+2 platemail, +2 large steel shield, +3/+4 vs. n'gathau bastard sword (Karelis), boots of leaping, gauntlets of ogre power, necklace of firebaubles* (8 uses).

Tactics: Lord Tork apologizes for his actions but attacks the characters relentlessly and ruthlessly, leaping around the fight to keep from being surrounded. As Lord Tork faces his eventual destruction, he regains a moment of control and the memory of his former life. He bequeaths *Karelis* to his most honorable opponent with the following words: "Take her and defend her as she defends thee, may you complete the task which I failed."

Unique Magical Sword

Karelis, +3/+4 vs. N'gathau Bastard Sword

This adamantine bastard sword is of magnificent craftsmanship, having a suppleness not normally seen in such a weapon. Its chiseled and engraved hilt is done in an ancient elven style, with a green dragon skin wrist thong attached to its star sapphire pommel stone. The emeralds adorning the cross hilt are embedded to appear like a pair of almond-shaped eyes of deep beauty and sadness. *Karelis* speaks abyssal, celestial, common, elven, sylvan, infernal, and the secret tongue of the n'gathau. She is imbued with speech and telepathy.

Karelis' is determined to destroy the horrid thing her body has become. Although her soul is trapped within the magical blade, Karelis' body lives on in the Plane of Agony. It is now a horrid, twisted, tortured being called a n'gathau. Neither the soul of Karelis nor Lord Tork are certain of the truth, but they suspect that Jhedophar sold Karelis to demonic creatures called the n'gathau in exchange for vile wisdom and great power. *Karelis* does not know the new name the n'gathau bequeathed to her body, nor does she even know what her body looks like after being twisted and tortured and reshaped by the ghastly rulers of the Plane of Agony. The sword's purpose is to lead heroes appropriate to the task to the Plane of Agony to destroy the n'gathau that Karelis has become, thus allowing her soul to escape the blade and go on to her eternal reward. The sword is +4 vs. n'gathau.

Spell-like abilities: at will—*detect magic*; 3/day—*detect evil*; 2/day—*protection from evil 10ft radius*; 1/day—*anti-magic shell*.

Note: If the characters somehow find a way to free Lord Tork from his servitude by gaining the golden circlet from Jhedophar, grant them a 1000 XP story award bonus. Should the characters cast *resurrection* upon the dust that was once Lord Tork, his ashes rise as a Lawful fighter in his mid-fifties. While wielding the fabled blade *Karelis*, Lord Tork is dashing and brave. Seeing the characters as great and noble allies, he offers to join them in defeating Jhedophar and Exeterus — if they then agree to travel with him to the Plane of Agony to seek the *Citadel of the Flayer Knights* where *Karelis'* body has been imprisoned for thousands of years.

Lord Tork, Male Human Warrior (Raised from Dead) (Ftr12): HP 67; AC –1[20]; Atk +3 *bastard sword* (1d8+3); Move 12 (30ft leap); Save 4; AL C; CL/XP 12/2000; **Special:** +2 to hit and damage strength bonus, multiple attacks (12) vs. creatures with 1 or fewer HD.
Equipment: +2 *platemail*, +2 *large steel shield*, +3/+4 vs. n'gathau *bastard sword* (*Karelis*), *boots of leaping*, *gauntlets of ogre power*, *necklace of firebaubles* (8 uses).

Treasure: The glinting metal in the chamber are *horseshoes of speed* that once belonged to Jasper.

What bit of memory still resides within the skull of Lord Tork remembers the sword *Karelis* well and prays that the soul within the blade may someday return to the elf maiden to whom it belongs. Although he attempted to do so in life, it was a quest he would unfortunately never fulfill.

L-7. Entry Hall to the Inner Labyrinth

An iron golem guarding the chamber leading to the inner labyrinth animates and attacks the characters instantly.

The portals to the inner labyrinth are 1ft-thick stone and held with *wizard lock* spells as well as being locked with mechanical locks.

Iron Golem: HD 16; HP 80; AC 3[16]; Atk weapon or fist (4d10); Move 6; Save 3; AL N; CL/XP 17/3500; **Special:** +2 or better magic weapons to hit, healed by fire (damage regained as hit points), immune to most magic, poison gas (10ft cloud, save or die), slowed by lightning. (*Monstrosities* 221)

L-8. Rue Mohrgs Morgue

Several vivisection tables greet visitors to this room. Dust-covered implements of torture sit on a bloodstained desk in the corner of the room. Complicated diagrams drawn in chalk on the walls detail various exploratory surgeries that once went on in this room.

This chamber is guarded by **3 mohrgs** that attack as soon as characters enter the chamber.

The mohrgs are made up of the bodies of greedy adventurers who sought to wrest the *mandrake staff* from Jhedophar but were destroyed and turned into morhrgs after hours of torture. Their treasures have long since fallen into other hands.

Mohrgs (3): HD 10; HP 76, 72, 67; AC 0[19]; Atk fist (1d8 + grab) or tongue (paralysis); Move 12; Save 4 (+1 in labyrinth); AL C; CL/XP 13/2300; **Special:** grabs and holds (automatic tongue damage, save escapes), paralyzing tongue (5ft range, –2 save or paralyzed for 1d6 turns). (*Monstrosities* 334)

L-9. One Wrong Turn

Stepping upon this floor plate triggers a **scything blade trap**. The blade swings down, attacking as a 5HD creature and dealing 2d8 points of damage to all characters in a 10ft space.

L-10. Nazoj's Chamber (or You're Not on the List!)

The demonic trappings of a fallen priest adorn this small chamber, and the ghost-like image of a being twisted with evil rises from the shadows. This is **Nazoj the demiurge**, who turns toward any priest or paladin and laughs cruelly. He asks, "So, are you on the list?" The creature looks over a parchment that crumbles to dust in its ghost-like hands. "No. It doesn't appear as if you are on the list after all. Truly too bad for you, but if you aren't on the list, Jhedophar says I have to kill you. I have fallen far in service to Jhedophar, so too shall you fall in the name of our dread queen Beluiri." With that, Nazoj shakes his head and says, "Besides, if you're not on the list, you're just not on the list." Nazoj then attacks.

Nazoj the Demiurge: HD 8; HP 52; AC 3[16]; Atk incorporeal chill touch (1d4 cold); Move 12 (fly 15); Save 7 (+1 in labyrinth); AL C; CL/XP 14/2600; **Special:** harmed only by cold-wrought iron or spells, incorporeal, magic resistance (50%), soul touch (save or die), transfixing gaze (30ft range, save or held for 1 turn as *hold person*). (*The Tome of Horrors Complete* 130)

Tactics: The demiurge uses his transfixing gaze on heavily armed and armored opponents so that he may use his soul touch ability to fly through them and slay them with ease. He next turns his attention to clerics and wizards to finish them off before they can harm him.

A doorway in the eastern wall leads to **Area L-18** of the inner labyrinth.

Treasure: The skeletal remains of three of the demiurge's previous victims bear the following items: a *ring of fire resistance*, a *cursed chain shirt* that appears as a +2 *chain shirt* but actually grants –2 penalty to the wearer's armor class, and a +2 *suit of chainmail*, and the *wardstone of Jhedophar*.

Note: The *wardstone of Jhedophar* allows free passage through the *wizard locked* doors of the Tower of Jhedophar without triggering any of the curses or traps upon them — with the exception of the doors to Jhedophar's personal chambers. Jhedophar left the *wardstone* with the demiurge as he knows Nazoj would give the stone only to someone who knows him well and is on legitimate business.

Lesser Miscellaneous Magical Item

Wardstone of Jhedophar

This enchanted flat stone bears a complex sigil and allows the wielder to unlock and bypass any of the *wizard locked* doors found within the lich Jhedophar's labyrinth and tower. The only doors the stone will not open are the Chamber of Divination (**Area 8-A**) and the lich's personal quarters (**Area 8-B**) within the tower. Otherwise, the *wardstone* opens the locked doors and bypasses any magical traps found on those portals.

Outside the tower and labyrinth, any class can use the *wardstone* to cast a *knock* spell 3d6 times before the stone becomes non-magical.

L-11. Lair of Exeterus

The stench of snakes and sulfur fill this huge chamber. As the light from the characters' torches stretches into the chamber, the glow reflects off a pair of great eyes burning like red-hot coals as they turn in their direction. Arcane chanting can be heard from the bowels of the chamber. Momentarily, a voice calls out to them:

"Who dares enter the lair of Exeterus and disturb his musings? Speak quickly, mammals, or I shall gleefully feast upon your paltry offerings."

At this point, **Exeterus the red dragon** partially reveals himself to the characters. The characters must talk or act quickly, or all is lost. Exeterus, like most of his loathsome kind, is a smart and deadly opponent. Should the characters impress Exeterus with the proper amount of pontification to his might and power, the red dragon makes his play, suggesting that the characters retrieve the *mandrake staff* for him. In return, he shall spare their meager lives.

If asked why he has not simply taken the staff, he scoffs and explains that the mighty lich Jhedophar has been too frightened to come down from his high tower and face the dragon's wrath. This is partially true. Jhedophar does indeed fear Exeterus, for he knows that while he could possibly destroy the dragon, the dragon has better than even odds of destroying him as well. Jhedophar figures that Exeterus makes a good guardian for his labyrinth, and so he simply ignores the upstart dragon. Should the characters agree to destroy Jhedophar and bring Exeterus the *mandrake staff*, the dragon tells them exactly where the key for all the doors in the tower and labyrinth is located (a *wardstone of Jhedopar* in **Area L-10** with Nazoj the Demiurge).

Of course, Exeterus has no intention of keeping his part of the bargain. Should the characters destroy Jhedophar, he greedily accepts the staff from them and then attempts to destroy them. Furthermore, should the characters attempt to sneak off without giving him the staff, he stops at nothing to hunt them down until one of them is destroyed.

Exeterus, Adult Red Dragon (10HD): HD 10; HP 40; AC 2[17]; **Atk** 2 claws (1d8), bite (3d10); **Move** 9 (fly 24); **Save** 5; **AL** C; **CL/XP** 12/2000; **Special:** breathes fire (3/day, 90ft-long cone, 40 damage, save for half), spells (5/4/3). (*Monstrosities* 139)

Spells: 1st—*charm person, detect magic, light, magic missile, read magic*; 2nd—*invisibility, phantasmal force* (x2), *web*; 3rd—*dispel magic, slow, suggestion*.

Treasure: Exeterus' treasure hoard contains the following items: a *+2 large steel shield*, a *+3 ring of protection*, a *cursed ring of spell storing (magic-user)* that actually reduces the number of third-level spells the wearer can use by half and casts illusions in place of the spells that the caster "thinks" they have cast (these illusions are seen only by the caster and his allies). All of the spells stored in the ring are cast as illusions. There is also a *staff of healing* with 23 charges, a *wand of ice storm* with 4 charges, a *+2 bastard sword*, a *wand of metal detection* with 44 charges, a *ring of three wishes* with one wish remaining, and a pair of *lenses of charming*. Exeterus also has 16,000gp worth of various coins, and 3450gp worth of gems, jewelry, and fine art.

Tactics: The vision the characters see when they enter is not actually Exeterus but a *phantasmal force* that the *invisible* Exeterus stands behind. If the characters make too much noise in **Areas L-11** or **L-12**, Exeterus is waiting for them when they arrive.

If the characters arrive looking for a fight, Exeterus breathes upon them. He follows by casting *slow* on lightly armored foes and *charm person* on heavily armored ones. Once he starts taking damage, he breathes fire when he can and seeks to slay one after another character until all of them are dead. Should any characters attempt to escape, Exeterus eventually discerns their location and mercilessly hunts them down.

L-12. Lartugi's Chamber

Lartugi was once a famous halfling thief who specialized in raiding and plundering the towers of several wizards throughout the world. That was until he took the left turn upon entering the labyrinth of Jhedophar and came face to face with Exeterus. Now, Lartugi is Exeterus' thrall, valet, and spokesperson when the dragon wishes to be left undisturbed. Exeterus keeps Lartugi constantly under the effects of charm and suggestion spells. He gave Lartugi some valuables from his treasure hoard to keep the halfling satisfied.

Lartugi, Male Halfling Burglar (Thf11): HP 33; AC 5[14]; **Atk** *+1 short sword* (1d6+1); **Move** 9; **Save** 5; **AL** C; **CL/XP** 11/1700; **Special:** +2 save bonus vs. traps and magical devices, backstab (x4), read languages, thieving skills.
Thieving Skills: Climb 95%, Tasks/Traps 85%, Hear 6 in 6, Hide 95%, Silent 100%, Locks 95%.
Equipment: *+2 leather armor*, *+1 short sword*, *potion of haste*, thieves' tools.

Lartugi is fairly intelligent but totally in the thrall of his dragon master, whom he defends to the death.

If the characters made lots of noise fighting the gargoyles in **Area L-14**, Lartugi hides and sneaks up to just outside **Area L-13** to observe the characters. Lartugi then slips behind them with his enormous hide ability and waits for them to meet his master Exeterus. Should the characters fight Exeterus, Lartugi remains in the shadows (and out of the way of Exeterus' breath weapon). If the characters take the deal, he tails them through the maze and tower, possibly aiding them as silently and quietly as he can while they fight Jhedophar.

Treasure: Lartugi, a thief through and through, hid his treasure (excluding what he carries on his person) within his chamber under a loose flagstone. In the hollow under the stone is a bag of gemstones worth 900gp and a sack with 100pp in it.

L-13. Watch Your Step

A pit trap hidden here is triggered by the first person to cross over the covering but doesn't activate until another being crosses. Thus, any scouts can pass over it with ease, but those following are in danger. Characters within 5ft of the character triggering the trap must roll below their dexterity on 4d6 or fall into the 60ft deep pit and take 6d6 points of damage.

A patch of **phycomid** grows upon the bones of a dead thief at the bottom of the pit. Among the thief's possessions are a set of thieves' tools and a *+2 dagger*. The rest of the thief's armor and equipment have long since rotted away. Casting *speak with dead* upon the thief reveals that his name was Yadre and that he was a servant of the infamous Underguild. His masters sent him to steal the *mandrake staff* in exchange for a promise of immortality.

Phycomid: HD 4; HP 24; AC 4[15]; **Atk** fluid globule (1d6 acid + spore infection); **Move** 3; **Save** 13; **AL** N; **CL/XP** 5/240; **Special:** fluid globule (20ft range), spore infection (hit by fluid globule, save or lose 1d2 constitution, and 1 constitution every 10 minutes thereafter until dead). (*The Tome of Horrors Complete* 430)

The phycomid fires its acid globule at the first victim to fall into the pit as soon as the character lands.

L-14. Gargoyles' Lair

This chamber is home to 12 four-armed gargoyles and a large margoyle known as Grytis. The 13 line the walls of the chamber, frozen, so that characters have a 1-in-6 chance to notice that the creatures are actually alive. Grytis and his brethren wait until the characters are in the center of the room to attack.

Four-Armed Gargoyles (12): HD 4+1; HP 30, 29, 27, 26, 23x4, 21, 20, 18x2; AC 3[16]; **Atk** 4 claws (1d4), bite (1d6), gore (1d6); **Move** 15 (fly 24); **Save** 13; **AL** C; **CL/XP** 6/400; **Special:** +1 or better magic weapons to hit, freeze (hard to spot). (*The Tome of Horrors Complete* 263)

Grytis, Margoyle: HD 9; AC 1[18]; **Atk** 2 claws (1d6), bite (1d6), gore (1d6); **Move** 15 (fly 24); **Save** 6; **AL** C; **CL/XP** 11/1700; **Special:** +1 or better magic weapons to hit, freeze (hard to spot). (*The Tome of Horrors Complete* 264)

Tactics: The gargoyles gang up on individual characters, with three groups of four attacking one character at a time, intent on destroying them. If the characters make lots of noise in **Area L-1**, the gargoyles cover themselves in *adherer oil* that Jhedophar gave them. Any character striking a gargoyle coated in this material must succeed on a saving throw or find that their weapon sticks to the gargoyle. The gargoyles worship Exeterus and make as much noise as they can while fighting. They may even disengage from combat to warn the dragon. For years, a disgusted Jhedophar has attempted to eradicate the gargoyles from the labyrinth's foyer, only to have them return whenever he is off visiting the planes of existence.

Potions

Adherer Oil

Adherer oil is the alchemically distilled secretion of an adherer. This milky glue-like substance is very sticky. When applied to a creature's body, it causes the blows of enemies' weapons to stick to their body unless their attacker is using a stone weapon or succeeds on a saving throw. Likewise, individuals coated in *adherer oil* gain an additional 1d6 added to their total dice for any grapple checks they make while thus coated. One application of *adherer oil* lasts for 3d6 minutes.

L-15. Entrance to the Inner Labyrinth

A pair of barrow wights guard the true entrance to the inner labyrinth. The barrow wights immediately attack.

Barrow Wights (2): HD 6; HP 45, 40; AC 3[16]; **Atk** slam (1d4 + energy drain); **Move** 12; **Save** 10 (+1 save in labyrinth); **AL** C; **CL/XP** 10/1400; **Special:** insanity gaze (30ft range, save or affected by *symbol of insanity* as spell), level drain (1 level with hit, slain creatures rise as barrow wights in 1d4 rounds). (*The Tome of Horrors Complete* 595)

A hallway to the southwest leads deeper into the labyrinth.

L-16. Death from Above

A pressure plate in the floor triggers a **falling block trap**. If triggered, the only true path to the labyrinth is permanently sealed off, requiring a *passwall*, *rock to mud* or some similar spell to bypass it. Any character within 5ft-by-10ft area of the falling block must roll below their dexterity on 4d6 to jump out of the way. Otherwise, characters take 6d6 points of damage as they are crushed beneath the stone.

L-17. E'elaim's Chamber

Once a sorceress and ally of Jhedophar, the **crypt thing** that remains is filled with spite and cruelty although it is not necessarily evil. E'elaim is bound to the power of Jhedophar for all eternity. She sits upon a throne fit for a queen, carved from brilliantly polished vermillion wood inlaid with gold and precious jewels. She uses her powers of teleportation to cast intruders from the entrance of Jhedophar's tower as she clacks her dusty jaws in a mockery of laughter.

E'elaim the Crypt Thing: HD 6; **HP** 43; **AC** 2[17]; **Atk** 2 claws (1d6); **Move** 12; **Save** 10 (+1 save in labyrinth); **AL** N; **CL/XP** 9/1100; **Special:** +1 or better magic weapon to hit, teleport other (save resists), turns as 10HD monster. (*The Tome of Horrors Complete* 114)

Tactics: E'elaim attempts to teleport creatures within 50ft of her in random directions throughout the labyrinth. She then flees into the tower to avoid the characters' subsequent assault, laughing hysterically all the while.

Treasure: The throne that the crypt thing sits upon is made of precious hardwoods and gold. It weighs just over 70 pounds and is worth approximately 700gp to a collector in a large city. E'elaim also holds a *wardstone of Jhedophar* she created on her own that opens all the doors in the labyrinth and the tower (except for the lich's quarters on the eighth floor).

L-18. False Entrance to the Tower

The doorway to this chamber is ornately wrought bronze and gives the impression that it is an antechamber leading to the foot of the Tower of Jhedophar. Halls lead off to the north and south, obviously skirting the tower itself. The door is warded with a **fiery explosion trap** that does 5d6 points of damage to any character within 20ft (save for half damage). In addition, the door curses the character fiddling with it to permanently lose 6 points of dexterity (save avoids).

Inscribed above the door is a warning that reads: "Turn ye back from the Tower of Jhedophar, or face his wrath, let one thousand curses blister your carcasses and burn your soul to ash and soot, and a thousand years may you suffer in torment for defiling his home! Be gone thieves this is thy last warning!"

This chamber beyond the doorway is the lair of **Clytos** the **gharros demon**. Beluiri gifted Clytos to Jhedophar as punishment when the gharros demon fell into her disfavor. Rather than destroy Clytos, she sent him to Jhedophar to do with as he wished. Of course, Clytos was recalcitrant and lazy. Having little use for Clytos other than as a guardian in his labyrinth, Jhedophar exiled the gharros demon to live within this chamber.

Clytos survived all these years by summoning dretches and devouring them when they found themselves trapped within the magic circle.

Clytos, Gharros Demon: HD 16; **HP** 117; **AC** –3[22]; **Atk** *+3 flaming battleaxe* (2d8+3 + 1d6 fire), 2 tail stings (1d8 + poison); **Move** 12; **Save** 3; **AL** C; **CL/XP** 22/5000; **Special:**

+1 or better magic weapons to hit, immune to electricity and poison, magic resistance (50%), poison (save or die), spell-like abilities, telepathy (100ft). (*The Tome of Horrors Complete* 143)

Spell-like abilities: at will—*darkness 15ft radius, mirror image.*

Equipment: *+3 flaming battleaxe (Suzette).*

Clytos bears a *+3 flaming battleaxe*. He calls the battleaxe "Suzette" as that is the name of the erinyes that Beluiri caught him with at a social event in the lower planes. Once the circle is broken, the demon intends to slay whomever he can in his rage at his long imprisonment. He does not leave the labyrinth, however; he knows that Jhedophar is likely to destroy him for doing so.

L-19: Crypts of the Barrow Wights

This chamber holds the crypts of 6 barrow wights who were Lord Tork's liegemen. They came to rescue his body from Jhedophar's clutches but failed miserably and now rest here as guardians.

Each barrow wight wears full plate armor and has a *+1 longsword* that it leaves inside its crypt. They emerge and attack as soon as characters enter.

Barrow Wights (6): HD 6; **HP** 46, 43, 41x2, 37, 34; **AC** 3[16]; **Atk** slam (1d4 + energy drain); **Move** 12; **Save** 10 (+1 save in labyrinth); **AL** C; **CL/XP** 10/1400; **Special:** insanity gaze (30ft range, save or affected by *symbol of insanity* as spell), level drain (1 level with hit, slain creatures rise as barrow wights in 1d4 rounds). (***The Tome of Horrors Complete*** 595)

L-20: Shadow and Shadow Rats Nest

This chamber contains a large refuse heap that once housed a large colony of rats. A shadow sent by Jhedophar to clean the labyrinth of any vermin eventually stumbled upon the rats' lair. Now, the shadow and his 4 shadow rat swarms — along with his 2 spawned shadows — wait in the darkness for their next meal. Feasting is good every few years when another foolish party of adventurers attempts to learn the secrets of the tower.

The dire shadow rats and the shadows attack when the characters enter the chamber.

Shadows (3): HD 2+2; **HP** 17, 15, 14; **AC** 7[12]; **Atk** touch (1d4 + strength drain); **Move** 12; **Save** 16; **AL** C; **CL/XP** 4/120; **Special:** +1 or better magic weapons to hit, strength drain (1 point strength with hit). (***Monstrosities*** 418)

Shadow Rat Swarm (4): HD 6; **HP** 42, 39, 34; **AC** 6[13]; **Atk** bite (2d6); **Move** 12; **Save** 10 (+1 save in labyrinth); **AL** C; **CL/XP** 7/600; **Special:** envelop, immune to fire. (***The Tome of Horrors Complete*** 535)

Treasure: Hidden among the detritus is a *+1 axe*, a *potion of healing*, and 344gp.

The Tower of Jhedophar

The following locations are found inside the wizard's tower at the center of the labyrinth.

1-A. The Entryway

The front door of the tower is 1ft-thick stone and held with a *wizard lock* spell. Hateful runes warn would-be thieves and trespassers away from the door.

Knock suppresses the *wizard lock* but does not protect the caster from the door's curse. Tampering with the door triggers a **curse** on the person fiddling with the door, who permanently loses 6 points of wisdom.

The entry chamber features a portrait of Jhedophar as he appeared in life. He is dressed in his caster's robes and bears a great staff carved in a grotesque and twisted mockery of a man. Several non-magical books are on a small coffee table, and a moldy green sofa and chairs sit around it. The chamber has no windows, and a doorway leads to the north. Several inches of dust coat the sofa, chairs, and the coffee table.

1-B. The Abjuration Chamber

The first floor of the tower is a room dedicated to the school of abjuration, a guard against any who would attempt to bypass Jhedophar's normal protections. Practitioners once studied spells here, but the thick dust on the floor indicates that such studies must surely have given way to the passage of time and neglect.

Runes are scribed on nearly every surface within this room, upon the tables and walls. Rune bindings and other symbols of protection and wards decorate scroll cases and bookshelves.

Unwarily perusing any of these volumes triggers a *ward of pain* upon the reader. The reader takes 6d4 points of damage unless he makes a saving throw for half damage.

Inside the Tower

Wandering Monsters: No wandering monsters are in the Tower of Jhedophar unless the characters let them in from the labyrinth. Instead, roll 1d10 for each level of the tower that the characters enter. On a roll of 1, Jhedophar is somewhere upon that level of the tower waiting for the characters.

Shielding: The Tower of Jhedophar is shielded from teleportation and dimensional travel "into" it. However, it is not shielded from teleportation "out" of the labyrinth. Jhedophar may enter and exit the labyrinth as he pleases, which is to say, he does not, traveling directly to his chambers in his tower and avoiding the goings on within the labyrinth altogether. The exterior walls are further shielded to be immune to the effects of *passwall, transmute rock to mud, stone to flesh*, and similar spells. Casting such spells "inside" the tower is fine, but they do not work on the walls of the outer tower.

Continuous Effects: Due to the shrine to Beluiri, the tower strengthens undead creatures dwelling within it, granting them a +1 bonus to saves.

Standard Features: Unless otherwise noted, all doors within the Tower of Jhedophar are locked and made of bronze. Nazoj the demiurge (**Area L-10**) and E'elaim the crypt thing (**Area L-17**) hold *wardstones of Jhedophar* that open all the doors in the labyrinth and the tower (with the exception of the lich's quarters on the eighth floor).

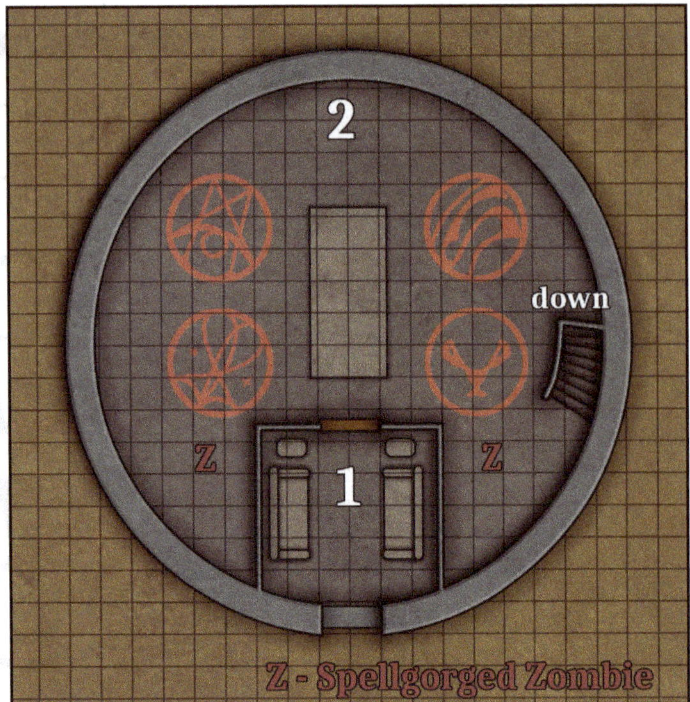

Two rounds after characters enter the abjuration chamber, **2 spellgorged zombies** step from the corners of the chamber and unleash a pair of *magic missiles* (4d4+4 points of damage, no save) before closing for melee. All of the spellgorged zombies found within Jhedophar's tower can cast the spells they store within them. Any special circumstances around these spells is noted in the creature's description.

Spellgorged Zombies (2): HD 2; HP 15, 12; AC 8[11]; **Atk** strike (1d8); **Move** 6; **Save** 15 (+1 save in labyrinth); **AL** C; **CL/XP** 4/120; **Special:** immune to sleep and charm, spell conflagration (20ft radius, 4d6 damage, save for half), store and release spells (*magic missile* [4d4+4 damage]). (**The Tome of Horrors Complete** 617)

A scroll case notifies Jhedophar if it is touched. After scrying on the characters in the labyrinth with his *crystal ball*, Jhedophar assumed they were dealt with and went about his studies. Once he learns the characters breached his tower, however, Jhedophar immediately prepares to face them. He immediately teleports to the evocation chamber (**Room 2**) and prepares to face the intruders.

One scroll case is a *scroll case of obscuring*. Within it are scrolls containing the following spells:

Scroll #1: *shield, hold portal, ESP*
Scroll #2: *invisibility 10ft radius, protection from normal missiles*
Scroll #3: *dispel magic*

Other scrolls and tomes are filled with various magical knowledge.

A staircase leads to a warded doorway that opens onto the second floor. The staircase is guarded with a message on the door to all that would intrude upon Jhedophar's stronghold:

> *Read in me and be relieved! Jhedophar has no time for thieves! With these words shall you burn. For your ashes, I have an urn.*

Reading this warning immediately sets off the *explosive runes* spell on the door. The spell does 4d6 points of fire damage to anyone within 10ft of the door.

NEW SPELL

WARD OF PAIN

Spell Level: Magic-user, 2nd
Range: Touched Item
Duration: Instantaneous

Deals 1d4 points of damage per caster level to any individual touching a chosen object (maximum 6d4 points of damage) as it imparts every ounce of agony and torture the caster can muster during the casting. Creatures making a successful saving throw suffer no damage from handling the warded object.

LESSER MISCELLANEOUS MAGICAL ITEM

SCROLL CASE OF OBSCURING

Much sought after by spellcasters, a *scroll case of obscuring* holds up to five scrolls of any level within its ebon-wood compartment. The scroll case is continually obscured so that would-be thieves and spells ignore the scroll case's presence. The case is especially useful for hiding secret documents a wizard or cleric does not wish his enemies to find. A character has a 5% chance per level of noticing the scroll case since it appears so innocuous.

2. EVOCATION CHAMBER

The evocation chamber is a bare room with a sand pit flanked by two low 10ft-high-by-40ft-long walls lined with engraved silver runes. Jhedophar created illusions here for those studying in the tower so they could practice their skills. He often created encounters for novices similar to what they might encounter on an adventure, thus allowing his apprentices to blast it out in the relative safety of this room. The walls are guarded against magic so that an accidentally miscast spell does not blow debris out into the well-tended flower gardens he once kept on the roof of the labyrinth.

As the characters search the room, a pair of **spellgorged zombies** attack, blasting the party with a pair of *fireballs* that deal 6d6 points of damage each, or half that with a successful saving throw.

After the fireballs explode, the zombies move forward and attack with their claws until destroyed.

Spellgorged Zombies (2): HD 2; HP 14x2; AC 8[11]; **Atk** strike (1d8); **Move** 6; **Save** 15 (+1 save in labyrinth); **AL** C; **CL/XP** 4/120; **Special:** immune to sleep and charm, spell conflagration (20ft radius, 4d6 damage, save for half), store and release spells (*fireball*). (**The Tome of Horrors Complete** 617)

The low walls flanking the sand pit are lined with traps that trigger a *phantasmal force*. For every 10ft section crossed, the traps create the image of a fire elemental. Up to 4 such illusions may be generated in this manner. Thus, if a character crosses 30ft across the sand pit, he triggers 3 *phantasmal force* **fire elementals**. The illusory fire elementals act and react exactly as if they were real. Casting *detect evil, detect magic*, or significant interaction allows a character to make a saving throw to disbelief the illusions.

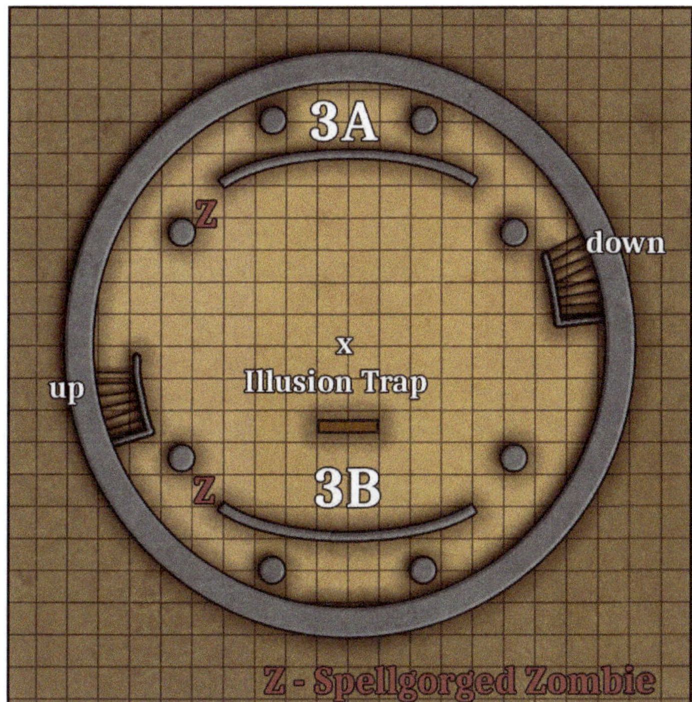

Fire Elemental: HD 12; **HP** —; **AC** 2[17]; **Atk** strike (3d8);
Move 12; **Save** 3; **AL** N; **CL/XP** 13/2300; **Special:** ignite
materials, immune to non-magic weapons. (***Monstrosities*** 156)

The staircase in the eastern side of the chamber leads down to the first
level. The staircase on the western side leads to the tower's third level.

A staircase around the edge of the room leads to a door on the third
floor. It is magically locked and warded, as are all the doors in the tower.

3-A. The Chamber of Illusions

The first task a practitioner of illusions learned from Jhedophar
was to tell the difference between illusion and reality. To that end,
Jhedophar constructed an illusionary maze on this floor of his tower.
Apprentices traced their way through the illusory walls to find the
staircase leading up to the tower's fourth floor.

Upon entering the chamber of illusions, **2 spellgorged zombies**
stalk the characters through the maze, ignoring any walls as they are
immune to the illusions.

Spellgorged Zombie: HD 2; **HP** 13; **AC** 8[11]; **Atk** strike
(1d8); **Move** 6; **Save** 15 (+1 save in labyrinth); **AL** C; **CL/
XP** 4/120; **Special:** immune to sleep and charm, spell
conflagration (20ft radius, 4d6 damage, save for half), store
and release spells (*disintegrate*). (***The Tome of Horrors
Complete*** 617)

Spellgorged Zombie: HD 2; **HP** 15; **AC** 8[11]; **Atk** strike
(1d8); **Move** 6; **Save** 15 (+1 save in labyrinth); **AL** C; **CL/
XP** 4/120; **Special:** immune to sleep and charm, spell
conflagration (20ft radius, 4d6 damage, save for half), store
and release spells (*cloudkill, magic missile* [4d4+4 damage]).
(***The Tome of Horrors Complete*** 617)

Tactics: One of the spellgorged zombies is set with a *disintegrate*
spell triggered to go off as soon as it is struck with a melee weapon.
Anyone striking the spellgorged zombie must make a saving throw or
the weapon is destroyed. Magic weapons add their enchantment bonus
to the save. This *disintegrate* spell functions once.

The other spellgorged zombie casts *cloudkill* followed by *magic
missile* (4d4+4 points of damage, no save) before closing to slam

opponents with its fists. The characters are unlikely to be affected by
the *cloudkill* spell, but the thick mists cause anyone within the room to
suffer a –1 to-hit penalty while the spell lingers for an hour.

3-B. False Staircase

Jhedophar created a partial staircase along the western edge of the
chamber of illusions. It extends upward about 20ft with the rest being
a permanent *phantasmal force* of a staircase continuing up to the
fourth floor. A character following the illusory stairs is considered to
be interacting with them and can attempt a saving throw to disbelieve
them. Those not disbelieving the illusion must roll below their
dexterity on 4d6 or fall 20ft to the floor below and suffer 2d6 points
of damage.

4. The Chamber of Enchantments

This floor has two rooms.

4-A. Still the Prettiest

This room is filled with mirrors and paintings, tapestries and murals.
One mirror is a mirror of charming. Since all the mirrors reflect one
another, anyone looking into a mirror must succeed on a saving throw
or become infatuated with his or her own image and be unable leave
the mirror's presence. They merely stand transfixed, brushing their
hair and reciting such phrases as "Still the prettiest," or "My, but
aren't I a fine one?" Characters must make an additional saving throw
if anyone tries to pull them away from staring at their image. If the
save fails, they become enraged for 1d6 rounds and attack their allies.

Standing in front of one of the mirrors is a **dwarf** whose beard has
grown so long that it curls upon the floor. He is so covered in dust that
he appears to be a marble statue.

Imbo the Undying was sent to the Tower of Jhedophar some years
ago on behalf of his benefactors to retrieve the *mandrake staff*. While
Imbo is a thoroughly evil dwarf, he may assist the characters should

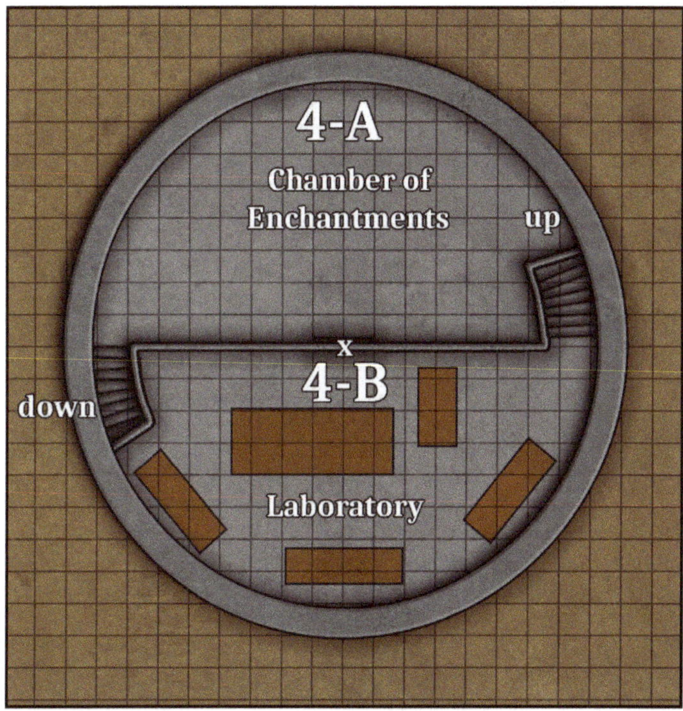

they break the enchantment upon him.

If freed, he helps the party up until Jhedophar is destroyed then betrays them at the first opportunity he gets to gain the *mandrake staff* for himself. Of course, in his berserk rage at being pulled away from the *mirror of charming*, he may "accidentally kill someone." If asked how he managed to survive so long without food or water, Imbo holds up a magical ring. While wearing it, he says, he didn't need to eat, drink, or sleep. He is lying, and the ring is actually a *ring of poison resistance*.

Imbo the Undying, Male Dwarf (Ftr5/Th6): HP 51; **AC** 4[15]; **Atk** *+3 warhammer* (1d4+9) or *+1 battleaxe* (1d8+7); **Move** 9 (18 with boots); **Save** 9 (+1, cloak); **AL** C; **CL/ XP** 11/1700; **Special:** +2 save bonus vs. traps and magical devices, backstab (x3), immortality (reforms after death), multiple attacks (5) vs. creatures with 1 or fewer HD, read languages, thieving skills.
Thieving Skills: Climb 90%, Tasks/Traps 50%, Hear 4 in 6, Hide 40%, Silent 50%, Locks 40%.
Equipment: *+2 leather armor, +3 warhammer, +1 battleaxe, boots of speed, gauntlets of ogre power, cloak of protection +1, ring of poison resistance.*

Roleplaying Notes: Imbo is as ruthless and bloodthirsty as it gets. Due to a particular curse upon his wretched soul, he cannot truly die, as none of the gods of the heavens or the dukes of Hell will tolerate his despicable presence among them for more than a moment. Even if disintegrated or reduced to ashes by the flames of a dragon, his essence remains and slowly reforms over time. He eventually returns — with slight gaps in his memory — as a stout and cruel dwarf. The reformed Imbo always seeks out the same style of weapons and gear, and always joins up with the cruelest and most powerful of allies. Imbo is an accomplished thief and liar and takes great pains to conceal his deceptions from the characters until the very last moment when he springs one of his particularly vile traps upon them.

Greater Miscellaneous Magical Items
Mirror of Charming

This ornate polished silver mirror is bordered in an intricately worked golden frame that makes it appear much like a boudoir mirror. It is roughly 5ft tall by 3 ft wide and affords anyone gazing into it a nearly full-length view of themselves. Upon gazing into the mirror, the viewer must succeed on a saving throw or become enraptured by his or her appearance, being unable to stop looking at themselves. Removing a viewer from gazing into the mirror forces the viewer to succeed on a second saving throw or attack anyone who disturbs the viewing for 1d6 rounds.

The chamber contains various bones antd dust-covered equipment of adventurers who starved to death in front of the mirrors. **Treasure:** A search of the bones and rotting equipment uncovers 1d4 random magic weapons and 2d100 gp. Jhedophar long ago gathered any magical items or gems from these failed intruders.

4-B. Laboratory

The second room within the chamber of enchantments is an alchemical laboratory with more than 2000gp worth of alchemical equipment. Several potions and bottles of unguents and reagents are found within this room. It is guarded by an invisible stalker that immediately attacks.

Invisible Stalker: HD 8; **HP** 60; **AC** 3[16]; **Atk** bite (4d4); **Move** 0 (fly 12); **Save** 8; **AL** N; **CL/XP** 9/1100; **Special:** invisible. (*Monstrosities* 265)

Treasure: Also found within this room are a *potion of animal control*, a *potion of heroism*, *potion of ethereality*, and a *potion of poison*.

A staircase leads upward to the next floor.

5. THE CHAMBER OF TRANSMUTATION

Jhedophar works out some of the most complicated forms of magic here, changing one object or item into another. The chamber is filled with benches and tables laden with items such as lead coins, small amounts of gold, rare gems, and the like. Several small cages and a large barred cell are in the corner of the room. The cages contain various creatures such as dire rats and pigeons. Several tools and gears are found in this workshop. If gathered, the tools are valued at 1000gp.

An **iron maiden golem** attacks any unbidden intruder entering the chamber of transmutation.

Iron Maiden Golem: HD 12; **HP** 50; **AC** 3[16]; **Atk** 2 slams (2d10 + trap); **Move** 6; **Save** 3; **AL** N; **CL/XP** 14/2600; **Special:** +2 or better magic weapons to hit, animate host (creatures dying inside golem turned into zombies), *confusion* (1/day, as spell), healed by fire, immune to most spells, slowed by lightning, trap (2 slams hit target, save or trapped inside golem, 20 damage/round). (*The Tome of Horrors Complete* 292)

The golem is programmed to trigger a *confusion* spell and then pummel to a pulp anyone attempting to cause it harm. If the golem is reduced to half its hit points, it is programmed to flee to Jhedophar's chamber of divination (**Room 8**).

A wand sits on a table. Beside it is a set of scales with a pile of gold and gems on one side and lead coins serving as a counterweight. *Detect magic* reveals the wand is magical, but it is **trapped** to polymorph anyone who touches it and fails a saving throw into a sheep wearing a blue dress. The wand is actually non-magical; a magical aura on it simply makes it appear to be so.

A staircase leads upward to a locked door that is the entryway to the sixth floor.

6. CHAMBER OF NECROMANCY

Upon entering this chamber, the characters find themselves face to face with a vrock demon flanked by a pair of spellgorged zombies. The vrock and zombies attack the party instantly with spells and spell-like abilities before closing in with melee attacks.

Spellgorged Zombie: HD 2; **HP** 12; **AC** 8[11]; **Atk** strike (1d8); **Move** 6; **Save** 15 (+1 save in labyrinth); **AL** C; **CL/XP** 4/120; **Special:** immune to sleep and charm, spell conflagration (20ft radius, 4d6 damage, save for half), store and release spells (*finger of death, magic missile* [4d4+4 damage]). (*The Tome of Horrors Complete* 617)

Spellgorged Zombie: HD 2; **HP** 14; **AC** 8[11]; **Atk** strike (1d8); **Move** 6; **Save** 15 (+1 save in labyrinth); **AL** C; **CL/XP** 4/120; **Special:** immune to sleep and charm, spell conflagration (20ft radius, 4d6 damage, save for half), store and release spells (*slow* [x2]). (*The Tome of Horrors Complete* 617)

Vrock Demon: HD 8; **HP** 57; **AC** 0[19]; **Atk** beak (1d6), 2 foreclaws (1d8), 2 rear claws (1d6); **Move** 12 (fly 18); **Save** 8; **AL** C; **CL/XP** 11/1700; **Special:** immune to fire, magic resistance (50%), spell-like abilities. (*Monstrosities* 105) **Spell-like abilities:** *darkness 15ft radius.*

In life, Jhedophar was no fan of raising the dead. However, since becoming a lich, Jhedophar has become a master of all things undead, even raising the bodies of his former apprentices as a new form of undead servant, the spellgorged zombie. Jhedophar taught initiates

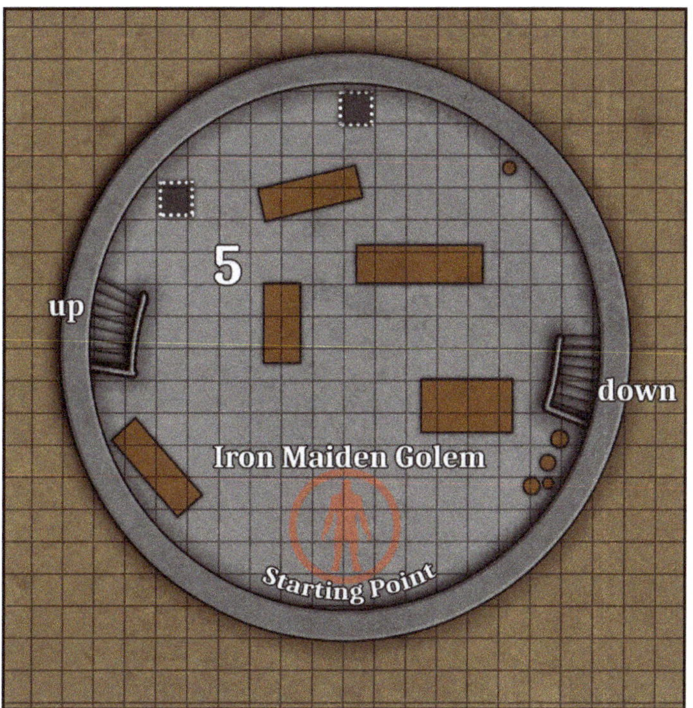

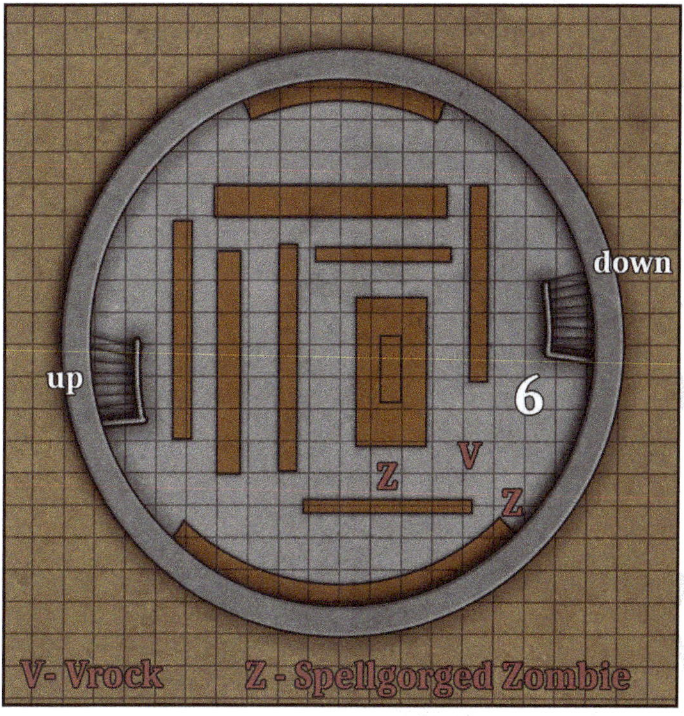

spells that only offered defensive possibilities and then only to a select and trusted few. All of this changed when Jhedophar dreamed of a beautiful temptress offering him immortality. He pored over his many eldritch tomes and finally sought out eternal life in un-death when he felt age creep into his bones.

Books and scrolls about the necromantic arts and defenses against the powers of the undead line the walls of this chamber, which is more of a library or a study than any other chamber in the tower.

A character searching the room for 1d6 x 10 minutes finds three scrolls of value:

> **Scroll #1:** *animate dead*, *disintegrate*, and *extension II*
> **Scroll #2:** *fear*, *polymorph other*, and *teleport*
> **Scroll #3:** *monster summoning III*, *telekinesis*, and *wall of iron*

7. THE CHAMBER OF CONJURATION

Binding runes are inscribed on the walls, doors, and floor of this chamber. Only high adepts were allowed entrance to this chamber where Jhedophar conferred with extraplanar forces in his magical research.

Guarding the chamber are **2 spellgorged zombies** triggered to summon allies to destroy anyone who enters the chamber unbidden.

Spellgorged Zombie: HD 2; **HP** 14; **AC** 8[11]; **Atk** strike (1d8); **Move** 6; **Save** 15 (+1 save in labyrinth); **AL** C; **CL/ XP** 4/120; **Special:** immune to sleep and charm, spell conflagration (20ft radius, 4d6 damage, save for half), store and release spells (*ice storm*). (**The Tome of Horrors Complete** 617)

Spellgorged Zombie: HD 2; **HP** 14; **AC** 8[11]; **Atk** strike (1d8); **Move** 6; **Save** 15 (+1 save in labyrinth); **AL** C; **CL/XP** 4/120; **Special:** immune to sleep and charm, spell conflagration (20ft radius, 4d6 damage, save for half), store and release spells (*magic missile* [4d4+4 damage], *monster summoning V* [vrock]). (**The Tome of Horrors Complete** 617)

Tactics: The first spellgorged zombie casts *ice storm* while the second summons a **vrock demon**.

Vrock Demon: HD 8; **HP** 61; **AC** 0[19]; **Atk** beak (1d6), 2 foreclaws (1d8), 2 rear claws (1d6); **Move** 12 (fly 18); **Save** 8; **AL** C; **CL/XP** 11/1700; **Special:** immune to fire, magic resistance (50%), spell-like abilities. (**Monstrosities** 105) **Spell-like abilities:** *darkness 15ft radius*.

A large magic circle is inscribed on the floor in the center of this chamber. Anyone crossing the threshold of the magical circle triggers a *magic mouth* that utters a **magical curse** in common in Jhedophar's raspy voice: *"Curious of magic, are you? Magic is a force to fear! Your courage fails you in the face of the arcane!"*

An old bard friend helped Jhedophar create this particular magical curse. This spell causes anyone prying around inside the tower uninvited who fails a saving throw with a −2 penalty to become deathly terrified of magic-users to the point where he or she runs in terror from anyone or anything perceived to be using magical powers. The affected character must thereafter succeed on a saving throw or become panicked whenever he witnesses a display of magic. The effects of this spell are permanent and can be removed only with *remove curse*. Unless cast by a cleric, this process terrifies the subject even more.

A staircase leads to the next floor of the tower. A locked and warded door enters the eighth floor.

Treasure: A *brazier of controlling fire elementals* filled with brimstone sits in the center of a magic circle. If Jhedophar is within hiss chamber of divination (**Room 8**), he can cause the fire to light and summon a **fire elemental**.

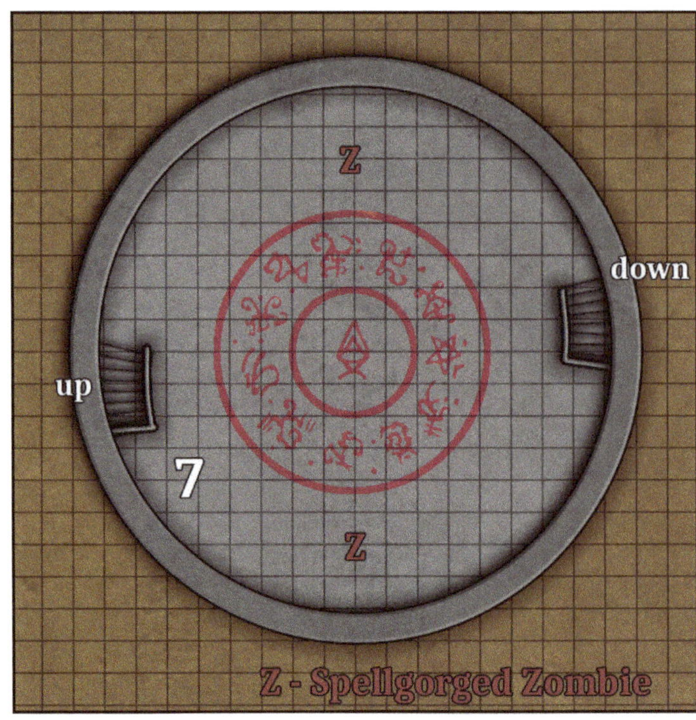

Fire Elemental: HD 12; **HP** 87; **AC** 2[17]; **Atk** strike (3d8); **Move** 12; **Save** 3; **AL** N; **CL/XP** 13/2300; **Special:** ignite materials, immune to non-magic weapons. (**Monstrosities** 156)

8-A. THE CHAMBER OF DIVINATION

This floor of the tower holds Jhedophar's private quarters. It is also where Jhedophar uses his *crystal ball* and *wizard eye* to spot troubles around the world and to seek the deeper mysteries of the universe from within and without the realms of existence. This special divination chamber is for Jhedophar alone to use; apprentices were never allowed entry here due to the level of concentration required for deep scrying. The room is filled with soft throw pillows and draped with velvet curtains. Several *gems of seeing* are on the pillows, and a large *crystal ball* sits on a gilt golden pedestal in the center of the room. A door to the north leads to Jhedophar's private quarters.

Unless already encountered elsewhere, Jhedophar finally reveals himself to the characters when they reach this room. He stands ominously before the characters, his bony hands clasped around the twisted length of the *mandrake staff*.

> This lush chamber is filled with plush pillows and shrouded in velvet curtains. Gems gleam from their place on the pillows, and a *crystal ball* reflects the light. A powerful-looking man stands before you, his bony hands clasped around the twisted length of a wooden staff.
>
> "My name is Jhedophar, and you must be powerful indeed if you seek to steal this twisted staff of root and flesh from me. But think first what you could gain instead if you wait a moment and listen to my parley."

If characters wait and listen to him, Jhedophar explains that the tower, the staff, and even all the treasures within his tower are worthless compared to his knowledge gained through centuries of researching the occult. In fact, he has grown tired of constantly defending the tower and is arranging to leave it altogether for a new place that is "a bit roomier" with a "more pleasant view."

But, Jhedophar explains, he has no intention of just "giving away" his belongings. He points out that a red dragon named Exeterus is now a squatter in the bowels of the labyrinth. If the characters are brave enough, they may be able to overcome the dragon, in which case he promises to give the tower to the characters. Jhedophar purposely does not mention the *mandrake staff* when he offers to hand over the tower. He has no intention of willingly giving up the staff. However, Jhedophar is very intelligent and understands that a large force of adventurers powerful enough to survive the traps and beasts within his lair may well be able to harm or even slay him.

Should the characters ignore his request for a pleasant chat, he reveals a *symbol of stunning* scribed upon a carved statuette of Beluiri sitting on his personal altar to his dark queen. The altar and statuette are hidden beneath a drapery of pure black silk that he keeps covered when entertaining "living" guests. Aside from the *symbol of stunning*, the altar of Beluiri is a foul and truly evil set piece to this otherwise lavish chamber. Jhedophar sacrificed each of his apprentices upon this altar and turned them into spellgorged zombies. Jhedophar cannot be turned while in its presence.

If characters attack (or if they reject his request),

he targets the characters with as many deadly spells as possible from his extensive repertoire before casting *teleport* and making his way to his new fortress upon the Plane of Molten Sky. He plans to work as an ambassador and spy for his dread Queen Beluiri.

Jhedophar, Male Half-Elf, Lich: HD 16; **HP** 117; **AC** −1[20]; **Atk** *mandrake staff* (2d6+3) or hand (1d10 + automatic paralysis); **Move** 6 (30ft leap); **Save** 3; **AL** C; **CL/XP** 19/4100; **Special:** appearance causes paralytic fear (4HD and below flee in terror), touch causes automatic paralysis (no save), spells (5/5/5/5/5/5/2/1). (***Monstrosities*** 294) **Spells:** 1st—*charm person, detect magic, magic missile (x2), read languages*; 2nd—*darkness 15ft radius, detect invisibility, invisibility, phantasmal force (x2)*; 3rd—*dispel magic, fireball, fly, haste, lightning bolt*; 4th—*charm monster, confusion, dimension door, polymorph self,* *wizard eye*; 5th—*animate dead, conjuration of elementals, feeblemind, teleport, wall of iron*; 6th—*anti-magic shell, death spell, disintegrate, project image*; 7th—*power word stun, reverse gravity*; 8th—*symbol*.

Equipment: *boots of leaping,* robes, *mandrake staff, bracers of defense AC 4[15], mandrake staff, ring of protection +3, cloak of displacement, rope of entanglement,* scroll of *flesh to stone,* scroll of *stone to flesh,* scroll of *power word blind,* scroll of *wall of iron,* golden circlet of skeletal warrior control.

If Jhedophar escapes, the characters might find themselves in a predicament if they previously made a deal with Exeterus. The red dragon most certainly expects the characters to return the *mandrake staff* to him or to be destroyed trying. They must either kill the dragon, or chase Jhedophar through the planes of existence, destroy him, and retrieve the staff lest Exeterus stalk them for the rest of their lives.

Tactics: Jhedophar has had plenty of time to prepare by the time the characters enter the divination chamber. He uses his spells to knock them down quickly, and attacks with his touch or the mandrake staff as needed. If the characters severely injure Jhedophar, he uses the *mandrake staff* to plane shift out of the tower to his new fortress in the Plane of Molten Fire.

In the event that the characters put Jhedophar on the defensive, he stamps the *mandrake staff* on the ground to activate it so it can attack on its own.

Note: At your discretion, Lartugi may step in to assist the characters if he was not slain previously. Alternately, if the characters are having too easy of a time with Jhedophar, Lartugi could join the fray as a wild card. If Lartugi still lives and Imbo is with the characters, Imbo switches sides, and he and Lartugi fight Jhedophar and the characters to gain the staff.

Treasure: 6 *gems of seeing* with 1d6 charges left each and a *crystal ball* with *ESP*. The golden pedestal on which the crystal ball sits is worth 1390gp.

8-B. Jhedophar's Private Chamber

Jhedophar's bedchamber contains a writing table with enough ink to scribe 20 levels worth of pages in spellbooks or 40 spell scrolls. Enough material spell components are in vials and jars here to cast each spell in his spellbooks six times. A locked secret door is behind

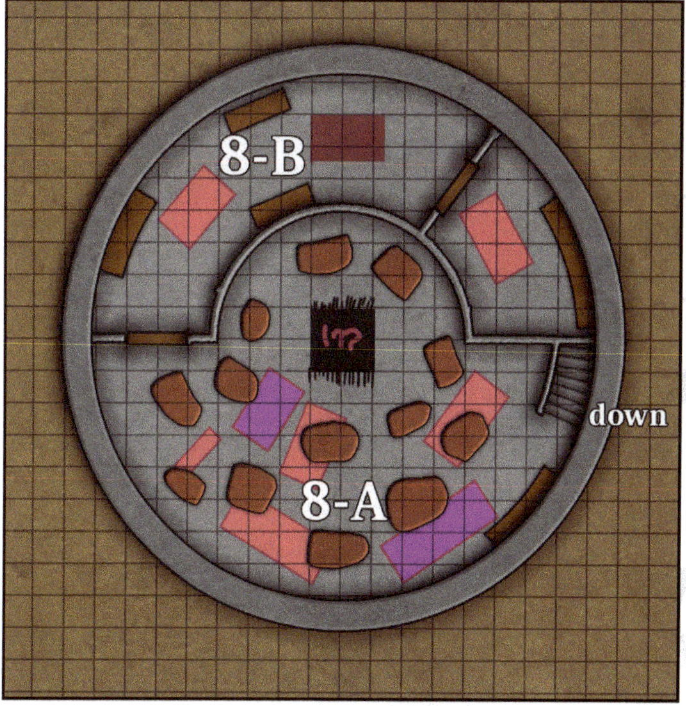

Staff

Mandrake Staff

This *+3 staff* is roughly 6ft long and nearly 3 inches thick. It is dark and twisted, having the vague appearance of a tortured, withered man. The top of the staff looks like the screaming head of a damned spirit. The staff does 2d6 points of damage with each strike.

Two times per week, a successful strike against a creature causes part of its body to wither. On a failed save, the limb shrivels and drops away (or the creature dies if the head was targeted). On a successful save, the creature still takes 2d6 points of damage from the intense pain. Withered limbs can be restored with *restoration, limited wish,* or *wish.* If a limb is not targeted, roll 1d6 to randomly determine where the strike lands: 1—head; 2—right arm; 3—left arm; 4—right leg; 5—left leg; 6—torso. Twice per day it can cast *passwall.* Once per day, it can cast *stone to flesh* (and its reverse), turn the wielder ethereal, and plane shift.

Once per week, the staff may be commanded to animate and walk about on its own accord for up to 1 hour. The staff sprouts a pair of root-like legs that allow it a movement rate of 12. The staff has AC 3[16], 32 hit points, and attacks using the wielder's attack roll. While the staff is moving independently of its master, it may use any of its special abilities.

an illusory wall. The door is guarded by a **fiery explosion trap**, *explosive runes*, and a **falling block trap**.

The fiery blast does 3d6 points of damage to anyone within 10ft (save for half damage). The *explosive runes* read "Look up!" and do 4d6 points of damage to the person opening the door. When the rune is triggered, it causes a falling block to drop. Anyone within 10ft of the door takes 5d6 points of damage if they fail to roll below their dexterity on 4d6 to jump clear.

A small chamber beyond the trapped door holds a staff, several robes, and a bookshelf that contains many different dusty volumes. Scroll cases line the top of the shelves, and a silver dagger hangs from a chain upon a hook.

An invisible bookshelf that contains Jhedophar's actual spellbooks. The other books are each trapped with a **fiery blast** that does 2d6 points of damage (save for half). Anyone attempting to read the books must make a saving throw with a –4 penalty or be struck by a *feeblemind* spell

Treasure: Jhedophar's spellbooks contain any spell you with to include. The pages appear blank, however, and require a spellcaster to cast dispel magic on each page to access them. Characters also find a solid silver *+2 dagger*, a *+2 quarterstaff* (cursed staff that animates and attacks wielder), a *wand of sleep* with 25 charges, a *ring of protection +1*, and 10 *potions of extra healing*.

Jhedophar keeps spare copies of his spellbooks and his phylactery hidden within a magical chest.

CONCLUDING THE ADVENTURE

If the characters made a deal with Exeterus and wrested the *mandrake staff* from Jhedophar, they must still return to face the red dragon. They could also try sneaking off with the goods. If the characters did not make a deal with Exeterus, the dragon notices the commotion from the tower and may be lying in wait for the characters when they attempt to leave. It happily extorts any treasure it can get from them as it decides whether to roast and eat them or to let them go.

The adventure concludes when the characters chase off or destroy Jhedophar and Exeterus. It is hoped they made it out with their lives and some new magic items and treasure. This adventure is not about completing some grand quest or accomplishing some great deed, it is about facing down danger and testing one's mettle against dangerous and deadly foes.

EXTENDING THE ADVENTURE

Exeterus and Jhedophar are great continuing foes you could use in your ongoing campaign. Perhaps the characters decide to hunt down Jhedophar in the Plane of Molten Sky or they find themselves stalked by the greedy dragon who uses innocent villagers as hostages as he burns and destroys all in his path to find the characters. This offers various roleplaying opportunities as the heroes are soon regarded as harbingers of doom. The story of villages being destroyed in their passing is passed along on the lips of bards and skalds until the characters final face up to the threat of Exeterus following them.

Jhedophar might also find the characters an amusing challenge and decide to torment them by popping into their lives from time to time. He might also use the characters to secretly do his dirty work. Jhedophar is extremely intelligent and quite selfishly despicable and unpredictable. Chaotic or Neutral characters may find Jhedophar to be a mentor or powerful patron to their dastardly deeds. Above all, Jhedophar is a survivor and seeks to stay that way.

Characters might also try to uncover the many secrets of the fantastic sword *Karelis*. The weapon seeks a strong hero who may finally free her body from imprisonment on the Plane of Agony.

APPENDIX A: NEW MAGIC

This chapter details new magic items found in the adventure.

NEW SPELL

WARD OF PAIN

Spell Level: Magic-user, 2nd
Range: Touched Item
Duration: Instantaneous

Deals 1d4 points of damage per caster level to any individual touching a chosen object (maximum 6d4 points of damage) as it imparts every ounce of agony and torture the caster can muster during the casting. Creatures making a successful saving throw suffer no damage from handling the warded object.

LESSER MISCELLANEOUS MAGICAL ITEMS

SCROLL CASE OF OBSCURING

Much sought after by spellcasters, a *scroll case of obscuring* holds up to five scrolls of any level within its ebon-wood compartment. The scroll case is continually obscured so that would-be thieves and magic ignore the scroll case's presence. The case is especially useful for hiding secret documents a wizard or cleric does not wish his enemies to find. A character has a 5% chance per level of noticing the scroll case as it appears so innocuous.

WARDSTONE OF JHEDOPHAR

This enchanted flat stone bears a complex sigil that wrapps around the rock. Any class can use the *wardstone* to cast a *knock* spell 3d6 times before the stone becomes non-magical.

GREATER MISCELLANEOUS MAGICAL ITEMS

MIRROR OF CHARMING

This ornate polished silver mirror is bordered in an intricately worked golden frame that makes it appear much like a boudoir mirror. It is roughly 5ft tall by 3 ft wide and affords anyone gazing into it a nearly full-length view of themselves. Upon gazing into the mirror, the viewer must succeed on a saving throw or become enraptured by his or her appearance, being unable to stop looking at themselves. Removing a viewer from gazing into the mirror forces the viewer to succeed on a second saving throw or attack anyone who disturbs the viewing for 1d6 rounds.

POTIONS

ADHERER OIL

Adherer oil is the alchemically distilled secretion of an adherer. This milky glue-like substance is very sticky. When applied to a creature's body, it causes the blows of enemies' weapons to stick to their body unless their attacker is using a stone weapon or succeeds on a saving throw. Likewise, individuals coated in *adherer oil* gain an additional 1d6 added to their total dice for any grapple checks they make while thus coated. One application of *adherer oil* lasts for 3d6 minutes.

STAFF

MANDRAKE STAFF

This *+3 staff* is roughly 6ft long and nearly 3 inches thick. It is dark and twisted, having the vague appearance of a tortured, withered man. The top of the staff looks like the screaming head of a damned spirit. The staff does 2d6 points of damage with each strike.

Two times per week, a successful strike against a creature causes part of its body to wither. On a failed save, the limb shrivels and drops away (or the creature dies if the head was targeted). On a successful save, the creature still takes 2d6 points of damage from the intense pain. Withered limbs can be restored with *restoration*, *limited wish*, or *wish*. If a limb is not targeted, roll 1d6 to randomly determine where the strike lands: 1—head; 2—right arm; 3—left arm; 4—right leg; 5—left leg; 6—torso. Twice per day it can cast *passwall*. Once per day, it can cast *stone to flesh* (and its reverse), turn the wielder ethereal, and plane shift.

Once per week, the staff may be commanded to animate and walk about on its own accord for up to 1 hour. The staff sprouts a pair of root-like legs that allow it a movement rate of 12. The staff has AC 3[16], 32 hit points, and attacks using the wielder's attack roll. While the staff is moving independently of its master, it may use any of its special abilities.

UNIQUE MAGICAL SWORD

KARELIS, +3/+4 VS. N'GATHAU
BASTARD SWORD

This adamantine bastard sword is of magnificent craftsmanship, having a suppleness not normally seen in such a weapon. Its chiseled and engraved hilt is done in an ancient elven style, with a green dragon skin wrist thong attached to its star sapphire pommel stone. The emeralds adorning the cross hilt are embedded to appear like a pair of almond-shaped eyes of deep beauty and sadness. *Karelis* speaks abyssal, celestial, common, elven, sylvan, infernal, and the secret tongue of the n'gathau. She is imbued with speech and telepathy.

Karelis' is determined to destroy the horrid thing her body has become. Although her soul is trapped within the magical blade, Karelis' body lives on in the Plane of Agony. It is now a horrid, twisted, tortured being called a n'gathau. Neither the soul of Karelis nor Lord Tork are certain of the truth, but they suspect that Jhedophar sold Karelis to demonic creatures called the n'gathau in exchange for vile wisdom and great power. *Karelis* does not know the new name the n'gathau bequeathed to her body, nor does she even know what her body looks like after being twisted and tortured and reshaped by the ghastly rulers of the Plane of Agony. The sword's purpose is to lead heroes appropriate to the task to the Plane of Agony to destroy the n'gathau that Karelis has become, thus allowing her soul to escape the blade and go on to her eternal reward. The sword is +4 vs. n'gathau.

Spell-like abilities: at will—*detect magic*; 3/day—*detect evil*; 2/day—*protection from evil 10ft radius*; 1/day—*anti-magic shell*.

www.ingramcontent.com/pod-product-compliance
Lightning Source LLC
Chambersburg PA
CBHW041204100726
47911CB00016B/862